CAN I KEEP IT?

LISA JOBE

PAGE
STREET
KiDS

THWUMP!

"Mom, if a squirrel follows me home, can I keep it?"

"A squirrel?
Squirrels like to climb trees
and gather acorns. . . ."

"If you were a squirrel,
where would you want to live?"

SCHLOOP!

"Mom, if a frog follows me home,
can I keep it?"

"A frog?
Frogs like to leap high and
splash in the water. . . ."

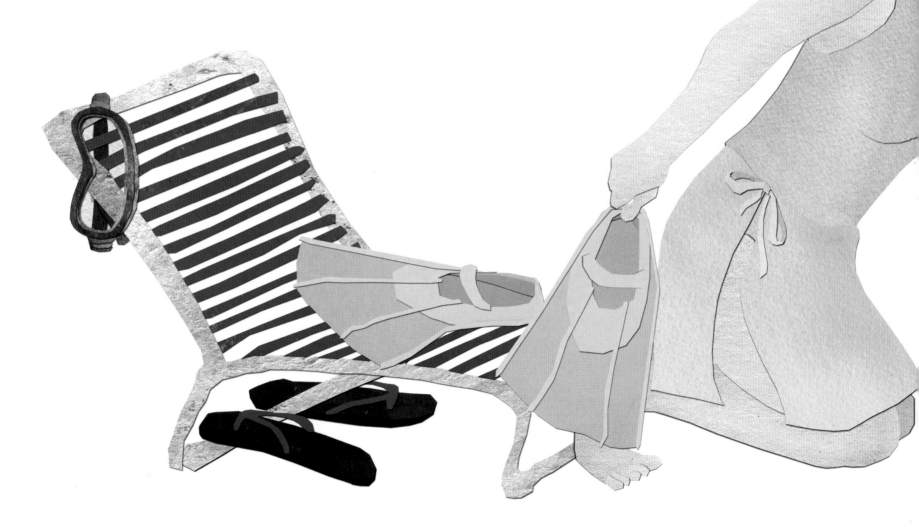

"If you were a frog,
where would you want to live?"

CLANK!

"Mom, if a bird follows me home, can I keep it?"

"A bird?
Birds like to build nests and
fly high in the sky. . . ."

"If you were a bird,
where would you want to live?"

"Cat!"

"If I were a stray cat
with a crooked tail,

where would I want to live?"

"Here . . .
with a boy like me!"

To Tisse and Wig,
for all your help along the way.

First published in 2019 by Page Street Kids,
an imprint of
Page Street Publishing Co.
27 Congress Street, Suite 105
Salem, MA 01970
www.pagestreetpublishing.com

Distributed by Macmillan, sales in Canada by The Canadian Manda Group

19 20 21 22 23 CCO 5 4 3 2 1

ISBN-13: 9781624146961
ISBN-10: 1624146961

CIP data for this book is available from the Library of Congress.

This book was typeset in Chelsea Market Pro.
The illustrations were done in watercolor, gouache, pastel, and digitally collaged.
Printed and bound in Shenzhen, Guangdong, China

Page Street Publishing uses only materials from suppliers who are committed to
responsible and sustainable forest management.

Page Street Publishing protects our planet by donating to nonprofits like The Trustees,
which focuses on local land conservation.